BAD WORDS

BAD WORDS

FEMINIST
QUEER
&
otherwise
RADICAL

SUSAN RUKEYSER

Printed in the United States of America
ISBN 979-8-9993343-0-5

Book design & cover photograph (Boron, CA)
by Susan Rukeyser

world split open press
Joshua Tree, California
www.susanrukeyser.com

For my son, Jeremy,
the best man I know.

let me stay tender-hearted,
despite despite despite

- Chen Chen, Twitter, August 9, 2020

CONTENTS

& otherwise **RADICAL**

WHY THESE 3 WORDS?

I chose the words "feminist," "queer," and "radical," to promote the Desert Split Open Mic, which I hosted in Joshua Tree, California, from 2019 to 2024, because I wanted those themes to shape our experience. Beginning under Trump's first term, the intention was to gather with other local writers who were moved, as I was, to more directly address social and political issues. It evolved from conversations sparked by *Feckless Cunt: A Feminist Anthology*, which I published as World Split Open Press in 2018. That book is a response to Trump and, more broadly, how it is to grow up and exist in our cis-het white patriarchy.

I perversely enjoyed that "feminist," "queer," and "radical," were all words that got under folks' skin. For different reasons, each was considered contentious, even controversial, by some. I hoped that would get us writing.

The word "feminist" took some hits from TERFs, or Trans-Exclusive "Radical Feminists," but there is nothing radical nor feminist about linking womanhood to genitalia or reproductive capacity. There is nothing radical about cruelty. Truly radical feminists dream bigger than any binary. They understand how different struggles for equality intersect.

Queer was a serious homophobic slur in the not-so-distant past, but now, for many, it is reclaimed as joy; possibility; a complete rejection of heteronormativity. Still, some worry that it threatens erasure of more specific labels.

It remains inherently radical to proclaim yourself feminist and/or queer, to risk mockery, harassment, or worse. But I wanted the Desert Split Open Mic to welcome all radical themes, including racism, gun violence, the climate crisis. I wanted us to explore radical new ways of writing.

The word "radical" is sometimes weaponized to frighten us into compliance, by those who benefit from the status quo. But what if radical just meant speaking up about what you were told to keep hidden?

Or claiming your own story so unconditionally that others see how they might heal, too? Radical is hearing and believing the stories of those we have historically dismissed or ignored. Radical is pushing through internalized shame, laughing off cringe, using your voice, and then stepping aside to share the mic. Radical is telling the truth, even in fiction, and always questioning the narrative.

I don't believe in "bad" words. The *Feckless Cunt Anthology* is evidence of my belief in the power of marginalized people to reclaim slurs used against them. To me, language is continually under construction and entirely within our control. Our ancestors built it, but we are responsible for upkeep. We can renovate, really tear the place apart.

Collected here are some of my favorite feminist, queer, and "otherwise" radical pieces of hybrid fiction and truth, prose and poetry. Each is short or very short, infused with the urgency I felt with the rise of Trump. Each is rooted in fierce love. Most were written for the Desert Split Open Mic, but some are older, and others brand new.

I believed in the Desert Split Open

Mic with my whole heart. It felt important, providing an opportunity for like-minded community to get more comfortable with the sound of our own voices, amplified, saying what we meant. The open mic helped crystallize my own purpose as a writer and improve my skills as a public speaker. I remain an introvert who rises to the mic when necessary.

Thank you for using your voice, even when it shakes.[1]

---

[1] Maggie Kuhn: "Leave safety behind. Put your body on the line. Stand before the people you fear and speak your mind – even if your voice shakes."

ALL I ASK (PROMISE ME)
January 2025

In a few days, inexplicably, a felon and the walking embodiment of toxic masculinity, a corrupt admirer of tyrants who inspired an attempted coup and said, "So what?" when a guillotine was wheeled out for his Vice President, will become President. Again. (Different VP this time.)

All I hope for us, as writers and people, is that we stay defiant.

I hope you will not tone it down or watch your language. Promise me you won't self-censor, that you will not obey in advance.

Tell me you won't avoid "bad" words, "sensitive" subjects, or "controversial" takes. Now, more than ever, you must write into discomfort and say what you mean, what we need to hear. In this (not so) funhouse mirror of Trump's

America, the bad guys won. All I hope for is that you consciously, deliberately exercise your right to free speech, that you flaunt your 1A rights as enthusiastically as they flaunt their AR-15s.

Free speech is precisely the hill I will die on. I am not strong by nature but by necessity. From the poem, "For strong women," by Marge Piercy: "Strength is not in her, but she/ enacts it as the wind fills a sail."

So many people are cowards. So many are not kind. For years, the bad guys have fought to remove books from school and public libraries, specifically books by and about BIPOC and LGBTQ+ people. Bad guys want to control the narrative. They defend this white hetero-patriarchy as if defending themselves.

They cannot silence us all. Promise me you will never silence yourself.

Ruth Bader Ginsberg said the national symbol should not be an eagle but a pendulum. I am pissed that it has swung back this way, again. Trump is, always was, that 80s-movie bully, the rich asshole who makes fun of nerds, poor people, people of color, queer people, people with disabilities, and women. He punches down, hard, for laughs.

Cruelty like that is so yesterday. I can't wait for the pendulum to swing back. We were finally getting somewhere. All I hope for is that we enact the strength to resist.

FEMINIST

A HYMN FOR US HERETICS

One bone-dry, summer afternoon, Poet and I sat together in the ruins of an abandoned homestead cabin, enjoying the Mojave Desert views from what used to be the window. Poet had a notebook and pen, but I had the words.

Poet said, "I want to write with fire."

"You want to write about fire?"

"No," said Poet. "I want to write with fire. I want my words to sizzle and combust into flames that fan out and singe the ears of anyone who needs them, bypassing those who don't get it. I want my questions to melt old ways of thinking – in my own head, first. I want my phrasing to be urgent and my subject matter, dangerous. I want my words to burn it down."

"Burn what down?" called Worry, from outside, where she waited so she wouldn't get in trouble for trespassing.

"Relax," I called back. "You know Poet speaks in metaphor."

To Poet, I said, "I wrote something, recently. I don't know if I wrote it with fire. It's a song of praise for girls of all sorts. A hymn for us heretics, maybe. It's dedicated to insistent girls, persistent girls, those who expect better and more."

"Get on with it," said Poet.

I cleared my throat:

"We do not have to smile for the bad guy who calls, 'Hey baby, hey beautiful… Hey where you goin, bitch?'

"Or for the good guy who explains what we already know and did not ask. Who says, 'Boys will be boys.'

"We do not have to smile for family that loves us 'anyway.' Or strangers who argue when we explain who we are.

"We do not have to smile to ease the tension. We do not have to smile to be safe.

"Not for well-meaning cowards who won't give themselves a hard look. Or some fool or another who says we're too much, or not enough, not what a girl should be, or a girl at all, in their opinion.

"We do not have to smile.

"Sing for the girls who tried to be President and the girls who voted for them, all of us awake from the dream of a savior patriarch. Those gunning for regressive backlash count on us relenting from exhaustion, softening back into compliance. I am tired; we are all tired. They want us to forget how righteous anger energizes. They want us to forget: The rights we *do* have were pried from their closed fists.

"No, we do not have to smile.

"Sing hallelujah for the girls fat as goddesses. Who fuck for experience and also love. Who disregard the opinions of assholes. Who dress for fun, who laugh hard, cry often, and always forget to shave. Who pretend not to notice when the wind lifts their skirts or their nipples against their shirts. Who were told to wear bras by gym teachers or their fathers: 'You're getting too old to walk around like that.'

"Sing for the girls who tell the truth, who came before and after us, with bodies like ours and different, with perspectives that resonate and others wholly new.

"Sing for the girls who grow to write with fire. We are beautiful in the light of it, these flames tended and stoked, generation to generation. In this light, we smile for real."

Poet was quiet for a while, after I finished.

Finally, Worry called, "I just think, if you're gonna call it a song or a hymn, there should be music."

I ignored her and asked Poet, "Did *you* hear?"

She nodded. She picked up her notebook and pen, the purple ballpoint we both liked.

"Okay," she said. "I'm ready."

BEAUTY STUFF

The child was a girl and, yes, that matters. She stared at herself in her mother's round, lighted, magnifying mirror, captivated by the green clay drying on her face. She was excited to finally be old enough to do beauty stuff. She looked like that witch from The Wizard of Oz. Ugly meant evil, everyone knew that.

The girl wanted to be beautiful, more than anything.

The mask stung, but her mother said that meant it was working. The back of the tube explained that this dermatologist developed, proprietary blend of spa-tested clays cleared and purified the skin, leaving it dewy and detoxified.

Yes, thought the girl. That's what I want. I want to be clean and beautiful and good.

On the edge of the bathtub, her

mother's round, yellow kitchen timer rang: *Brrriiing! You're free!*

Finally, the girl wet a washcloth and scrubbed away the hard, green clay. She rinsed her face and patted it dry, then reassessed herself in the mirror. Her usually pinky-beige skin was red from stinging that had *not* eased in a minute or two, as the tube promised.

Her skin looked tighter. Not beautiful, though, after all that. In fact, now that she really looked at herself, hard, she couldn't believe how ugly she was. She would have to try another mask.

INGROWN RAGE

By twelve years old, my legs were too long. I was taller than the boys, so I slouched, because girls should be small, I was told. Petite, waiflike, a pocket Venus, the girl shorter than the boy, even if she must bend her knees or wear flats when she wants to stilt-walk. In high school, the cutest, tiniest cheerleader was thrown into the air as if weightless, as if nothing, and oh how I wished I was small enough to be thrown around, how I wished to be less.

Just wait till the boys grow up, I was told. No man ever complained that a woman's legs were too long, I was told. It was assumed that I wanted attention from men. Needed it. It was assumed that I, all girls, exist in relation to men. Our legs are for them, as are we. Girls aren't asked if they mind being inspected for their suitability to this tired old system, and we are all deficient: too big, too dark, too short, bag of bones, fat ass… She has her dad's face, poor thing… a man's nose, but we can fix that… we can tame that bad hair. If she would just stop biting her nails and dress like a girl… put some mascara on those pale lashes. She could make an effort for chrissake, smile once in a while. No man wants an angry woman.

But rage is a rational response. Rage, like the furrow in my twelve-year-old brow, learning: women are one thing and men another, and if men want to fuck you, if they can tolerate you, you will be safe. Safer.

Rage, like the cords in my neck, tight from a lifetime of stooping, which remind me of the strings on the cello I held between my twelve-year-old legs. The cello demanded passion and fidelity but did not push beyond my knees.

Rage, like the ingrown hair on the legs I still shave because the women men want to fuck, the women men can tolerate, have legs smooth as plastic, I was told, and my fifty-year-old legs are closed to men… finally. But it is hard to unlearn the rules.

Rage, like the ingrown hair that

never tried again, but coiled in on itself, festering and stuck in these hot pink lies we are all told. It did not grow as intended, up and out, into air, light, the world.

Rage, like the ingrown hair finally extracted by clean tweezers, unfurling up and out, into air, light, the world; angry fluid draining from a hot pink mess that I wipe away like it was nothing.

HIS VENUS

A year ago, Dana was fat in a fertility-fetish sort of way. Her tits bloomed over her belly, her belly swung down to her knees. In her museum guard's uniform, she was reliably squat.

A year ago, Dana was flushed with euphoria, a startling new lust. Dwight worked in Pre-Columbian, cataloguing new acquisitions. He had developed a thing for the voluptuous female form.

"Occupational hazard," he joked as he buried himself into her, as greedy for her as she'd ever been for buffalo wings or chocolate. She liked soft centers best, buttercreams and caramels.

Dwight said he'd found his Venus. He moved himself in. Dana noticed some of her neighbors grinning at her that day. One of them even said *Congrats.*

She was a source of life, Dwight said.

"Just look at yourself."

He told her to undress, then stood behind her at the mirror. He put his hands on her stomach, between her thighs. She hated watching herself like this, but if she was what he wanted—? She tried to close her eyes, but he said No.

He breathed into her ear, "God, your hips."

Dwight said he had powers. He communicated with all biology, his own sperm included.

"I'll let them know it's time," he said.

A year ago, she believed. There was no real reason she *didn't* want a baby, and his hands felt good. Soon she was just as greedy for him. Her skin bristled as he moved onto her, into her.

In the mornings, before driving them to work, he fried eggs. Dwight stood naked at the stove. As he cooked, Dana thought of the museum's Greek and Roman statues with their hard white marble thighs. Solid thighs, immovable.

Dwight wanted everything from her. He told her how to give it. She'd never had that and was so grateful. On the drive home from the museum, Dwight stopped for burritos, burgers, buckets of meat. He'd grab bags of cheese popcorn, chewy fruit candy, pizza and cookies and chips.

"Eat," he insisted, pushing plates toward her.

Dana was bigger each week, but not from a baby. Dwight said he would have a chat with her fat cells, get her ovaries on board.

Dwight started filling up the house. He brought home secondhand toys and baby clothes, because any day now Dana's body would obey. He found a bouncy swing at Goodwill and hung it from their bedroom doorway. Dana couldn't squeeze past but was too ashamed to say. She started sleeping in her recliner, but not well.

"Pig," Dwight muttered one evening as he placed a bowl of spaghetti on her TV tray.

He was mad, but she did not know why. It had been over a week since he'd wanted her, and she burned for his fingers, for his weight on her.

"That food's going to waste?" he snarled.

She dug in her fork.

Dwight perched on the last clear

section of couch. Stacked between them were piles of stuff he'd bought, then forgot. He watched her eat.

The museum fired Dana when she was caught dozing in the sculpture garden. Her legs just weren't up to all the walking anymore. Decorative Arts did her in.

Dwight didn't like to be disturbed during the workday, so she took a cab home. At the front door she took a breath, pulled in her belly and turned sideways, inched her way inside. The hallway was especially difficult, crowded with Dwight's latest purchases: a filthy old stroller, a crib mattress, a playpen with rusted hinges, and a collection of stuffed bears, matted and spilling their guts. Items had tumbled into the path to her recliner. She climbed over them as best she could. A stack of picture books toppled down. Dana rubbed her shoulder, wondered what Dwight saw in junk.

Months later, still no baby.

Dwight hardly touched her anymore, hardly went near her, and Dana was relieved. On her ankles and heels were sores she could not reach. One night, she didn't get the bedpan under her in time.

Mortified, she screamed at Dwight,

"You never told my body anything!"

He did not say a word, just handed her the phone. Dana couldn't turn around, but she knew. He was gone.

Men with saws cut their way inside. Every point of entry was blocked by garbage, they said. She heard the word "uninhabitable" They removed a ragged square of wall, then stepped into her living room. The EMTs loaded her onto a gurney and wrestled her out of her mess.

The night air took her breath, all that sky. The moon was a hard white stone.

"Thighs," was all she could say.

The EMTs laughed, said she must be hungry for chicken.

Dana felt her neighbors spying from behind curtains. Of course they stared, she didn't blame them. Just one year ago, Dana was fat in a fertility-fetish sort of way, a shiny round Venus flush with lust.

SPRAY TANS IN THE 70s

When LuAnn turned eleven, she hit the wall.

"Eleven is when it happens," LuAnn says, to the stylist teasing her daughter Amber's hair into a high, shimmering web.

Amber turned eleven a few months ago. Now she puckers her lips so LuAnn can dab on more pink lipstick.

"You go one of two ways at eleven," LuAnn says. "Now, Amber, she went cute."

The stylist laughs, like maybe LuAnn is kidding, but Amber is beautiful – that is as obvious as the stylist's big brown mole, squatting behind her ear like a troll. Does she think a little hair hides that much ugly?

The summer LuAnn turned eleven, 1976, pageants crackled with Bicentennial spirit. Dresses were red, white, and blue, trimmed with patriotic bunting. Hair was bleached a dazzling, All-American blonde. They set waves with orange juice cans, curled face-framing ringlets. Lip gloss, sure, but not full makeup like nowadays. No spray tans.

"I cringe," LuAnn says, "when I think how good I coulda looked."

She pokes the corner of Amber's eye, secures a wayward false lash.

Amber is spray tanned an exotic, caramel brown, darker than her natural shade. That's the Latin in her, only thing she ever got from her father. Just as well; LuAnn didn't want to know him, once morning broke and she sobered up. He mumbled something like, *You're on the Pill, right?* and she kept her mouth shut. Already, she felt her daughter beginning inside her, just a little more beautiful, thanks to this stranger's DNA.

LuAnn knows she isn't much to look at, not since she turned eleven.

"Glitz!" Amber says, panicky. She grabs her mother's wrist, shoves the watch into her mother's face.

LuAnn doesn't take things too personal on pageant days. As they head to the stage for the Glitz portion, LuAnn hands Amber a Pixy Stix.

"Big smile," she coaches.

Amber takes a breath before going on, extends her arms to frame that skirt. Her music starts and she walks out, faces the nearly empty hotel banquet room. The judges sit at a table in front of the stage. A man with a deep-woods Georgia accent reads into a microphone: "Amber enjoys swim team and playing with her new puppy," although Amber didn't make the team this year and the puppy is now a dog they keep chained up out back. Amber says he stinks real bad.

LuAnn heads out into the audience, to an empty row of chairs near the back. Amber poses and pulls her lips into a smile. LuAnn considers now that Amber may be a little long in the leg to wear this sparkly dress with its high crinoline pouf.

Suddenly, Amber hesitates. She looks to LuAnn. The music is playing, but Amber is frozen. LuAnn moves to the aisle and demonstrates the routine she choreographed and Amber knows. She knows it by heart! LuAnn thinks, I have to do everything?

LuAnn did her best, that summer of 1976, when she hit the wall. She tap danced with little American flags and smeared Vaseline on her teeth, to smile big as Farrah Fawcett Majors. But it was hopeless: her forehead rose up in bumps, her belly developed a pot. Her nose grew into something from the old country.

"Some girls outgrow pageants," a judge at the Touch O' Class Pageant told her mother when they left, again, without a crown. LuAnn knew what that meant.

Sometimes, humiliation rises like a noxious cloud, and you think it will choke the air right out of you, or maybe you just wish. At Touch O' Class, LuAnn kept going, kept that greasy smile. It wasn't till later, on the long drive home to Valdosta, that she bawled. Mama leaned forward, worrying at the dark through the windshield, her thumbs twitching on the steering wheel. When LuAnn grew tired of crying, she stared down at her shoes, silver tap shoes with ribbons for laces. LuAnn loved those shoes, has them still, in a box.

Now, Amber recovers and picks her routine back up, following LuAnn's lead. But her face is tight, and that smile is a grimace. When the music ends, Amber exits with a curtsy that can't undo the damage.

"I know," she whispers at LuAnn, as she joins her in the audience. She plops down onto a folding chair, crushing the crinoline. "And, my luck, Genevieve's next."

Rumor was, Genevieve's aunt was second runner up, Miss America 2004.

Genevieve took ballet and did this thing with her neck, looking over her shoulder at the judges. When she walked onstage, she went to work. She had a trademark wink.

Amber says, "They should go ahead and give her Grand Supreme right now. Will anyway."

"Genevieve won't forget her routine," LuAnn snaps, and Amber winces. Good, thinks LuAnn. Finally got her attention. Amber's lack of focus is frustrating, because can't she see? Amber has a shot! She went cute.

"But cute isn't enough," LuAnn whispers, not looking at her daughter. "Cute evaporates, like that!" She snaps her fingers, causing a woman a few rows up to swing around and glare.

"I have talent," Amber pouts.

"Oh, honey," says LuAnn, as she watches Genevieve dance and wink her way to first place. She feels Amber's humiliation rise, a hot, choking cloud. "Genevieve has Talent all locked up."

LuAnn could have done better, that summer of 76, even with pimples and a nose like her grandfather's. Maybe if she'd had her daughter's caramel skin, not this bluish white, which she keeps out of the sun or freckles bloom in smudges? If they had spray tans in the 70s, and LuAnn was just a little more beautiful? Like Amber, but wanting it more, working harder?

Genevieve finishes her routine to scattered applause. LuAnn sneaks a look at her daughter. Maybe now she won't put up such a fuss about rehearsing. You can get by on cute for just so long, thinks LuAnn. Sooner or later, you lose.

Just like me, you lose.

A STORY OF BLOOD THROUGH ME

A Story

At thirteen, I was convinced I would be the very last girl in my seventh-grade class to get her period. I was thirteen, for god's sake, and *still* not a woman!

How embarrassing.

Every morning before Homeroom, the pretty and most popular girl, Sloane, took a poll:

"So… who got their period since yesterday? Seriously, Susan, not yet?"

About a month later, I was finally able to tell Sloane, "Well, I got it."

"What?" she said. "Oh, we're not doing that anymore."

Of Blood

I remember how it was. Every month, the blood. Usually met with indifference, or relief, or disappointment. For women, just the way it is. We don't talk about it much, but blood unites us.

I remember how it was when I was pregnant. I was older this time, my son already eight and eager for a sibling. (With him, I bloomed with happy pregnancy. I delivered without drugs. I felt invincible. I thought, I should do this for other women. Be a surrogate for those who want babies but, month after month, see nothing but blood.)

I remember how it was when blood came when it shouldn't. In week ten, the embryo becomes a fetus. It looks like a comma: big head, a curve of body. Just over an inch long, the size of a kumquat. If it's wished-for, it's a baby.

First, just a hint, then undeniable pink. Then red, bright with shame. I staggered to the bathroom, all of me pouring out.

Through Me

What they don't tell you about menopause is much of anything. Sure, you see hot flashes on TV, moms fanning themselves for laughs, when the truth is no joke:

Sudden, sickening heat surges up into your neck, your face, and your body goes instantly slick with sweat. It courses from beneath your breasts, your arms, down your spine; but you don't let on, because that might make people uncomfortable.

How embarrassing.

So you hide what is happening inside you, as you have hidden – so well, so often – the truth of your female body, like it is no big deal, and you are not undergoing a protracted, alchemical transformation. Again.

Then, just as suddenly, you go cold, damp, and shivering.

Menopause is exhausting, and you will feel deflated and old, sometimes, and at others, fiercely powerful, your blood reclaimed, your battle-worn body liberated. You may rage at everything or cry and cry. You may bleed more before you bleed less. You may be ravenously horny or alienated from your own body. Again.

(If thirteen-year-old Susan thought blood made her a woman, what does she think I am now?)

What they don't tell you about menopause is how long it takes for the blood to leave you. Your periods may become irregular, erratic. They may stop and stay gone for the better part of a year, only to come roaring back like some unwelcome guest who cannot take a hint, like you did not already say your goodbyes.

When you have had enough, some wise crone may advise you to buy a multipack of tampons or pads. The idea is that the universe loves a prank and will respond by immediately ceasing your periods forever. The first multipack I bought didn't work, but the second one did.

You can donate the leftover period products to people who need them, younger people. You will start to notice how many people are younger than you.

What they don't tell you, but I will, is that it does get harder, the older you get, to forgive this country its betrayals, disrespect, and cruelty, how this blood makes our bodies the government's business.

I am freer, without it.

I visualize red blooms of relief for younger people desperate for them, ruined underpants happily sacrificed as proof of an empty womb and no choice to be made, in this post-Roe absence of choice.

And if I do occasionally mourn the blood that represented possibility and felt like hope? Blame it on my hormones, still settling after another protracted, alchemical transformation.

FOR SALE: BLACK & BLUE BABYDOLL (USED)

$4.99, panties N/A

First of all: I am not ashamed. I turned forty and my husband left me for an older woman. He was characteristically thoughtful and apologetic: It wouldn't be fair to *me* if he stayed, because he was pretty sure Rosie was his soulmate.

It was nothing against me.

Hell yes, I bought myself slutty lingerie after that! I hoped that life had something left for me, too.

This babydoll nightie has structured, underwire bra cups, royal blue satin overlaid with black lace. They lift and jut your tits – sorry, boobs – like trophies. Useful if you're trying to get someone's attention, but not what you'd wear to relax.

The matching G-string panties are

long gone, and that's a long story. Let's assume you wouldn't want them.

The nightie has adjustable satin shoulder straps and a big black rose, smack dab between the boobs. Sheer black mesh hangs from the bra top to the hips, the edges finished with a band of silky material. It's parted in front, like a curtain. Lets you break it to him slowly, LOL.

Or her, I guess. Do women go for this kind of stuff? I wore it for men, but don't let me limit your imagination.

The first guy, I met at the gym's smoothie counter. I'd just finished a Zumba class, and the endorphins made me chatty. I asked if all green smoothies taste like lawn clippings and he replied,

"My wife and I are separated."

It just dropped out of him, like that. I made him wait in the den while I changed into the nightie.

Then I called, "Come join me in the bedroom," like we were in a movie.

He lost his mind when he saw me. LOST HIS MIND. It's probably worth more than $4.99.

Sure, it felt odd, when that first stranger walked into the pale blue bedroom

I had shared with Stéffan, or when he peeled back the comforter and slipped in on Stéffan's side. But then, and ever since, the room was different. The present replaced the past.

At the beginning, my heart flopped when Stéffan walked in the room, that kind of love. We tried to make a baby. We'd get our hopes up, and then there'd be silence where there should be a beat, or blood where there should not be.

We stopped trying.

Some things run their course. Silence becomes the language. It is not uncommon. Too many marriages hollow out. Former lovers lie next to each other without touching. There is nothing lonelier.

Divorce *is* death, don't let anyone tell you otherwise.

I wore this babydoll for five men, once each. I'm selling it because I am ready for something a little less rough on the tits – sorry, boobs. Give these forty-year-old girls a break, already. I think I'll still find men who want to sleep with me, even if I am comfortable.

Forty is old enough to know that once you become who you are, there is no going back. My husband left, and I don't have a baby, and all week I answer phones so other people will seem important, and then on Friday nights, I hit up a dive for cheap frozen daiquiris and let middle-aged men flirt with me. They need stuff, too. I'm happier than I remember being. I have secrets and some color in my cheeks.

Forty isn't old, but it's not exactly young. You start to get a sense of how quickly time passes, how little time is left, comparatively. You have some regrets, by forty.

But, wearing this nightie, with its aggressive bra top, I forgot regret and remembered myself. With those five kind strangers, I felt like the best, bustiest, most bodacious beauty queen they had ever had the good fortune to encounter. I heard my own laugh for the first time in forever. For an hour or three, they were mine. Then I sent them away. It was bliss, which makes up for a lot.

I'm asking five bucks. Trust me, you will get your money's worth. Serve up your tits – no, I do mean tits – and get what you need. Go ahead and set the rules. Wear slutty lingerie with strangers or with your soulmate, what do I care?

Everybody needs something.

Maybe what you need is this black and blue babydoll.

THE PROOF IN HER GUT

The woman was fifty-one years old when she swallowed a pen. She told her husband and her doctor, at the time, but they did not believe.

She thought she saw a spot on her tonsils. She wanted a better look, she told them, so she used a plastic, felt-tip pen to hold down her tongue. Somehow she lost her balance, and the pen slipped right down her throat.

Twenty-five years later, the surgeon who finally retrieved the pen from her stomach reported that she had "a blameless medical history, other than well-controlled depression."[1]

He wrote "hello" with the pen, to prove that it still worked, despite stewing

---

[1] Waters, et al, "An incidental finding of a gastric foreign body 25 years after ingestion" (British Medical Journal, 2011)

in stomach acid for a quarter century. Someone took a picture that was posted and reposted around the internet.

"Isn't it amazing!" many people exclaimed.

Yes, I thought, isn't it amazing that when this seventy-six-year-old woman awoke from anesthesia, she did not scream, "I told you so!"

When it happened, her doctor took an x-ray but did not see what she insisted was there. I imagine the look of concern he exchanged with her husband. I imagine the woman stoic and dignified, raised to be agreeable, to put aside her anger. As if she did not know exactly what slipped inside her own body. As if she did not know what stayed.

I think about that first night back home, after the doctor's x-ray failed to support her claims. I imagine the woman sleepless beside her husband, the pen and her anger settled deep into her belly. She knew he considered her a liar, delusional, or, at best, confused. It had to be one of these.

How many more nights *were* there, for them? Did they divorce years ago, or are they married still, apparently happy, and it's only when you look deep into her old-woman eyes that you see the shadow of deferred rage?

For twenty-five years she was not believed about her own body, her own experience, as if she did not carry the proof in her gut.

Isn't it amazing that she did not write, *Fuck you!* with that pen, once the surgeon had his fun?

Maybe, over those twenty-five years, the woman came to doubt her own story. It did sound preposterous. It was only when the pen was retrieved and photographed that she remembered: She had always known the truth. She should have trusted herself. Isn't it amazing that she was gracious, or so I imagine?

I wonder if they sent her home with that felt-tip pen. What story might she write with it? Or was it written already, inside her?

YOU WERE THE GIRL WHO

You were the girl who didn't brush her hair. All summer, barefoot in the marshy woods behind your house, wearing those red shorts, because the high school boy who did yard work for the Delucas watched you, when you did.

You drew everything. Our comfy Connecticut town was the world's least interesting place, but you were going to be a famous artist in New York or San Francisco, you hadn't decided.

You threatened to run away all the time, and that terrified me, the idea of you not here. You said it so often that finally I wasn't scared anymore, just sad. Because if you could leave like that, I knew you didn't feel the same way.

You thought I was funny. You wanted to teach me to shave my legs, but I was embarrassed.

That was the summer my parents split, and I got my period, but didn't tell my mom, only you. Out in the woods we shared a beer, if you were able to sneak one. On an oak stump, you made a little altar to Gaia, votive candles and empty beer bottles and roses snipped from the Delucas' yard, and a locket some boy gave you, maybe that high school boy. We made up rituals, our eyes closed, hands clasped in the flickering candlelight, inhaling the forest, exhaling gratitude.

When the mosquitos got bad, we went inside, down to your basement bedroom where I admired your drawings. You watched me, doodled on your thighs, because it drove your mom crazy. There were sketchbooks all over the floor, pages scrawled with whatever you were working on: horses, getting their proportions right, and boxes that appeared to have weight. Noses seen straight on, I remember you did a lot of those. And hands – you said hands were the trickiest body part.

Your school notebooks were covered in ink, your textbooks, too, although you knew you'd be fined. Sometimes we took Polaroids of each other. Once, we slipped off our shirts first. More than anything, I wanted to be you.

You were the girl who got kissed by lots of boys because you always kissed back, curious. I think you went all the way with that high school boy, but you never said.

You were the girl who had an abortion. Junior year, you carried condoms in your purse, but Steve asked, "Don't you wonder how much better it is, natural?" And you liked the sound of that, natural, and you were the girl who was curious. But you got pregnant, and Steve was going nowhere, but you certainly were, you were leaving the world's least interesting place. Steve got his next girlfriend pregnant, too, another girl who was the girl who had an abortion.

After you moved into Brooklyn for art school, I saw you just that once, at Stew Leonard's. You said you were back in town for Sandy's wedding, and I said, "I didn't know you two were friends!" And you said, "I'm the Maid of Honor."

We were strangers. It shocked me, how suddenly we were.

That night after Sandy's wedding,

you were at your parents' house, in your old basement bedroom, alone. You were the girl who moved away just like she said she would and found an interesting life and became more beautiful. I was in my apartment over Murphy's Tavern, far from the woods, wondering if you'd ever been my best friend, or did I make that up?

They said you slept through the whole thing. How did they know that?

A sixty-foot-deep sinkhole opened up beneath your parents' house, swallowing the basement. The police put up tape and kept everyone out, even your parents. The structure was unstable. The sinkhole was expanding. News vans parked along your road.

Eventually, there was a press conference: "The victim is presumed dead." They were not able to retrieve your body. They used the word "entombed."

You were the girl who made our town interesting.

I imagined you pinned by rock somewhere down deep in dirt, wrapped in your bed sheet like a shroud. I imagined you rotting back into Earth, cradled by Gaia through that most natural transformation.

You were the girl who could never leave. How did they know you slept through it?

Demolition crews took apart your house piece by piece, recovered what valuables they could. They filled the sinkhole and dumpsters with everything else. A chain link fence went up around the condemned property. The lawn gave way to weeds, the driveway fissured. In time the marshy woods spread, consuming your grave.

You were the girl who fell into Gaia's arms in the world's least interesting place. You were the girl who drew black ballpoint on thighs scratched and filthy from the woods.

I was the girl who looked for you in drawings like kaleidoscopes, fragments arranged in patterns recognizable for a moment, then collapsed, shifted into something new.

QUEER

FOR SALE: BABY SHOES, VERY WORN[1]

As is.

Of course you'd rather buy new baby sneakers. Pristine, with unmarked soles that still light up. I get it. I'm doing an eighteen-year stretch as a "stay at home" suburban mom: the lone brown face at HOA coffee mornings. I get how the little humiliations turn you petty. But, by now, you know: parenthood means adjusting your expectations. What I have here is a pair of dirty, creased, size 4 Little Mermaid Baby Girl sneaks, white with glittery accents in purple, aqua, and silver.

I took a women's studies course in college – I don't need the problematic gendering of baby shoes or the appalling sexism of "The Little Mermaid" explained to me, thanks. Yes, Ariel gives up her voice. But she wants those legs. She wants that

---

[1] "For sale: baby shoes, never worn," a famous 6-word story misattributed to Hemingway

man. Ariel knows: no one gets everything. It's not her fault that The Walt Disney Company insists on happy endings.

These sneakers were cheaply mass produced overseas, and it's probably best not to think about that too much. American parents rely on products made by workers who are not paid enough. You couldn't afford most crap, otherwise. I know what you're thinking: participation is complicity. When you buy into consumerist culture, you discount your integrity. The blood is on your hands. Yeah, well, guilty. But I have news – so are you. We were born complicit. We don't get to have cool, cheap stuff and feel good about it, too. So go ahead, consume. Hold your nose when you have to. Post on social media about how much you hate capitalism.

What I mean is: your baby is filthy. She was born that way. A smelly mess at both ends, most of the time. But that's life, and if babies do anything, they grab you by the collar and bring you in for a good, hard look at life. Maybe you managed not to think about the sticky reality before a baby squeezed her way out into the world and looked up at you like you'd know what to do. We suckle and shit, grab and hit, laugh when other people fall down.

We are animals, but worse.

The point is, your baby needs shoes. And you don't want to spend a lot, because who has a lot to spend? And she'll just grow out of these sneakers, sooner than you think. Seriously, you'll be lucky to get a few months out of these. They're dirty, but then so is your kid – I'm sorry, but it's true. And that's good, that's what you want. You want her in sneakers already battered by this rough world. From the moment of her conception, this world was hers.

Or his.

The baby girl who wore these sneakers is now a teenaged boy. I guess he was never a girl. His dad and I misunderstood from the start. We announced that we had a daughter, as if it was up to us to say who she was.

Who he is.

I get everything wrong, but I am trying. Cristian's dad went silent. He will talk about the weather or what he had for lunch; sometimes his job: conference calls, too much paperwork. Never his son, who used to be his daughter Cristina, who switched around the last two letters of her name and became himself, as if happiness can be that easy, as if it should be.

(My husband is only a couple of years older than me, but less flexible. It happens, with age, if you're not careful.)

I'm selling these sneakers to show Cristian: "I get it. I chose a costume for you, before you were old enough to tell me to go to hell." Before he could walk without stumbling, I pulled sparkly Little Mermaid Baby Girl sneaks on his feet and then I secured the Velcro.

He liked them, at the time. He braced himself against the couch and belly laughed as he stamped his feet and made the soles light up.

Which they don't anymore, sorry.

They will protect your kid's feet. She – or he – has a long walk ahead on this planet. She will make her way among fellow humans hopped up on corn syrup and noise, guns and panic. Isolated animals who lash out when cornered, often sooner. Who won't compromise. Offense is the best defense and stand your ground and he fit the profile and she should've known better. Your child will swim in overheated oceans, ingest plastic, and survive. She will stumble into gutters strewn with broken glass, bleed, scar, and live on. The best a parent can do is mitigate the damage.

Your kid needs shoes. They don't have to mean anything. Your child is here to teach you, too. He will tell who he is, in time. You have to be patient. And flexible. And ready to let go, anytime.

ANOTHER VERSION OF MYSELF

from The Worst Kind of Girl (Red Light Lit Press, 2025)

Sky and I lay across her futon where we'd ended up, sweaty and spent. The room was in the back of Sky's queer roller disco, The Rainbow Roll. It was dark except for twinkle lights around the window and the moonlight streaming in.

Sky rolled over to the upturned crate that was her nightstand and retrieved a small paperback book.

"Check this out," she said.

The cover was an x-ray of someone's neck. The vertebrae were twisted and out of alignment. Printed across the cover, in a font meant to resemble a doctor's messy handwriting, was the title, *Blue,* and the author's name: I.M.

"I.M. is that poet who came to the open mic, the one with the big, blonde hair? It's their first book, a mini collection – a chapbook, I think they called it? Their publisher wants to rent the Rainbow Roll for a reading and launch party. Isn't that cool?"

"Very cool," I said, opening the book.

The poems were just a few lines each, the words spaced across the page, as if the desert winds blew around and between them. I flipped through, reading lines here and there that caught my eye. There was a recurring image of a child sitting alone on a split rail fence, watching.

"It's from a queer publishing collective in the Coachella Valley, and it sounds like they could help us draw younger skaters from down the hill."

I said, "Well, the desert is everywhere in these poems. And it's queer because I.M. is, I guess?"

"Not just because of that," Sky said. "That's her neck, on the cover. Shit, I mean their neck. I need to do better with pronouns. The young queers are impatient with their elders, not like I blame them. What do you think?" she asked. "I.M. wants to do a short reading and signing. I figure that's your department."

"Why?" I said, sitting up.

"Because you are my favorite local queer writer."

"I'm not—"

"Maybe you need to give yourself permission to be imperfect. To do it wrong, or messily, or too slowly."

"To do what?"

"Everything," she said. "Give yourself permission to do, say, and be everything wrong."

I said, "It's not just that I feel dishonest, calling myself a writer."

"I figured."

"You keep calling me queer."

"Yes."

"All my life, I called myself straight."

"You're still worrying about this?" She reached out to stroke my arm. "Babe, you are definitely not straight. Not anymore. What will help you accept that?"

Why was I having trouble? Did some small part of me not want to be gay, or bisexual, or whatever I was now? No, truly. That wasn't it.

"I think it's about identity. About having to move into a whole new identity at age fifty, just when I was settling in for the long haul, thinking I knew myself a little. Something like this makes me wonder if I knew anything."

In Sky's bathroom, I looked into the

mirror and whispered, "Queer. Paula, you are queer." I repeated it a few times, to get myself used to the sound of it.

It felt… okay. Clearly, I could not go around calling myself straight anymore. "Queer" felt closer to the right word for myself – if a word must be found – than "lesbian." Hadn't I disqualified myself from that? I couldn't see myself using "pansexual," since I'd only just learned what it meant. To me, it felt grandiose. I was just a fifty-year-old woman, with a past full of men, who fell in love with a woman. "Bisexual" seemed old-fashioned, like people were one thing or another, but I had long since stopped believing that anything was black or white. Everything was shades of gray. Or hues on a spectrum. Fifty years of life had made me humble. Maybe each of us was a blend, in varying proportions, of everything a person could be.

Queer it was, then.

I could not resist the smile on Sky's sweet face. She watched as my thoughts churned. She waited and stroked my arm. Sky trusted me when she had every reason not to. How could she not worry that I was a straight lady having a midlife crisis? Experimenting, or taking a temporary break from men, toying with her heart?

I wondered then if I had made it clear enough to Sky, how much I appreciated her trust, how deeply I felt about her. How sure I was. I vowed to treat her like a queen and never leave her.

I said, "I.M. could read from the book for, say, twenty minutes. Give us some context, the backstory, how she—"

"They."

"Shit, sorry. How they came to write these poems, the inspiration for the collection, and then we could get into their thoughts about the high desert's gay scene."

"Don't say 'gay scene,'" said Sky, trying not to laugh.

"Okay, what it's like to be queer in the high desert. And then maybe we could have an open mic and invite people to—"

"It all sounds perfect. This is your thing, Babe. I want you to do it your way. I'll take care of the skate party afterward."

I snuggled up close to this woman I loved, who took it for granted that I was capable of things I had never imagined, of being someone new.

My heart flopped around every time I was near her. I felt like I understood Sky, and she understood me. And she loved me anyway.

It made me uncomfortable, sometimes, how she searched my face for the girl I once was, before men looked at me and I felt them looking, before I let them make my choices, before I hitched shame to my belt loops and let it drag me down.

I wanted to say, "That girl died before she was born."

With Sky, I was another version of myself, again. We talked about how it was, to be women in a man's world. To be diminished. We talked about definitions and labels and how sometimes a person just wants to be, as they are, without explanation.

"Thank you, Sky," I said, grabbing her hand and bringing it to my lips for a kiss. "I mean it. For seeing me the way you do. I never would have dreamed. I'm having so much—"

"Fun?"

I nodded.

"Right on," she said.

"You're opening up new worlds for me," I said.

"Speaking of opening up…"

She reached for me, and we kissed,

and I was gone.

Sky trusted me, so I would trust her, and this, how my body responded, how my heart flopped around. Again, despite everything, I would trust this hope I felt.

L IS FOR LATE TO THE PARTY, BUT I HAVE SOME NOTES

A is for Ally. Plural: Allies. Used in a sentence: "Not all queer people are queer allies."

B is for Bodily autonomy, whether abortion or gender affirming healthcare.

B is for Bisexuals, clowned on by both gay and straight people. Hashtag, not all gay and straight people.

(See also : **P** for Pansexuality.)

C is for Compulsory heterosexuality, or comphet, named by Adrienne Rich, referring to society's pressure to be straight, if at all possible, discouraging us from exploring our sexuality.

(See also : **R** for Regret.)

D is for Drag queens and kings, brave beauties who play with gender as if "feminine" and "masculine" and are just roles for actors and we are all in the cast.

F, as in Fluidity. What if nothing is fixed?

G is for Gay, of course, which used to mean joyful and still does.

I is for Intersectionality. If your feminism, or your queerness, is not intersectional, it is shortsighted.

L is for "Love is love," which means nothing. Straight love is not the standard to which queer love aspires. And all love is *not* equal. Some love is toxic. Some love is insufficient.

Maybe **L** is for Longing or Lust.

No, **L** will always be for Lesbians, creators of an alternate, anti-patriarchal, cooperative vision of home, work, and womonhood; feminine power unburdened by a desire for men.

M, as in Misogyny.

(See also : **I**, for Internalized.)

Q is for Queer, proof that slurs can be reclaimed.

R is for Race and Reproductive freedom, inherent to any discussion of oppression.

T is for Trans beauty, detached from the binary's expectations.

T is for Transphobia, a violent response to the unfamiliar. What if we just believed what people told us about themselves?

T is for TikTok, where I landed in search of Book Tok, allegedly the future of book promotion. But soon I was watching short, heartfelt videos of women discussing the challenges of coming out "later in life." Like me, many of them wondered if anyone understood how hard it is.

One thing I learned on TikTok is that "later in life" means "in your 30s." And hashtag "later in life" is often followed by "lesbian." I watched TikToks by women who realized they were never attracted to men, who had denied their feelings for women, who felt shame. That wasn't me.

Others said, "Men were just easier. Men were always around." Now that rang a bell. They spoke of patriarchy, heteronormative culture, and the privilege of passing for straight. Yes, I thought, all of that.

W is for Women, hairs pricked like prey.

X, as in stop. **X** as in *no*.

Y, as in Yes. Yes to sitting with discomfort. Yes to life bringing what change it must.

Z is for Generation Z. Raised on a poisoned planet, with active shooter drills, they are exuberantly queer. They expect acceptance, like we all should.

May they rewrite all the old stories with new language.

ID, PLEASE

"How do you identify?" is a question I was asked recently, a question I was never asked before.

I fled to the desert to live out my days as a hermit and instead fell in love – with a woman. I had not considered that my identity might change. Did it have to? Were there rules? Alas, I am notoriously bad at following those.

Now I am asked to select a letter for myself from the expanded but still limited menu. So I consider: How DO I identify?

I identify as an animal, hominid, advanced primate.

I identify as a creature of base impulses, greed and spite, and I identify as a highly moral person.

I identify as a socialized human being who used to try harder to do things the "right" way, who identifies as a feminist because the "right" ways are the tools of our oppression.

I identify as a writer and the child of journalists, an enemy of censorship, policed language, black and white thinking.

I identify as a woman who recognizes the woman in any human being who claims it.

I identify as a human with female reproductive parts, who has known the relief and agony of blood, who desperately wanted and did not want to be pregnant, at different times. I identify as a mother. I know I was supposed to say that one first.

I identify as a mother who believes a woman's body is entirely her own business. Everyone's body is entirely their own damn business.

I identify as an angry woman who cannot understand why we are not all angry.

I identify as someone who used to call herself a straight ally. Who discovered the absence of fear at a women's music festival and returned every summer for eight years, who recognizes that what women can be, do, and look like is an infinite spectrum.

Who knows the words to several songs by the Indigo Girls, drove three

Subarus, and adopted eight cats (not all at once). Who was told by a gay coworker that she was "the straightest lesbian" he'd ever met.

I identify as someone who used to say, "I wish I could love a woman, but it's impossible, due to my stubborn heterosexuality."

I identify as someone who overcame that.

So, now, if I MUST identify myself with a letter, I choose Q. The letter Q looks like a big friendly face with a jaunty moustache, an oval roomy enough to hold us all as we move together towards a better future.

Because, progress may be slow and too often thwarted, but it is inevitable.

I identify as a reclaimed slur.

And with love, and hope, and fear, and courage, and more, so much more. Just like everyone else.

WATCH ME SIZZLE AND SPIT

Since I came out later in life (much later than my 30s, sorry kids), I've encountered some whack digs at my sexuality.

At first I listened too reverently to women who had been out longer, internalizing their jokes and bad takes. I wrote a whole novel about a 50-year-old woman who falls in love with a woman, after a lifetime of men, and how she reckons with that. *The Worst Kind of Girl* is infused with questions I found myself exploring. I was fresh off a friendly, sexy relationship with a man when I fell hard for a woman, so hard I believed we were meant to be.

But this did not cause me to realize I was a lesbian, that I'd been one all along, as many do, prompting the social media hashtag, #lateinlifelesbian. Nor did I realize that I was actually straight, and had been all along, when my first sapphic relationship blew up like a SpaceX Starship rocket (and others failed to launch).

For me, it was never a question of "or," but "and." Like *The Worst Kind of Girl*'s protagonist, Paula Winger, I initially settled on "queer," because it allowed for fluidity and the space to explore, to expand, rather than contract. A few years in, I tried on "bisexual," but it felt antique, dusty with a stubborn adherence to a binary I don't believe in. I know many, especially younger, bisexuals argue for expanding the definition of "bisexual" to include attraction to all genders, and goddess knows I'm always in favor of stretching our elastic language to allow for progress.

But, in my case, a more accurate word already exists: pansexual. My adult son jokes that declaring oneself pansexual is akin to ordering the sizzling fajita plate: you don't hate the attention! We laugh about that, but lately I'm owning it. I see bi and pan people as helpful evidence that human beings exist on a spectrum of sexuality, as we exist on a spectrum of gender, and other spectrums as well.

None of this challenges your identity unless it does. As Dorothy Parker allegedly said, "Heterosexuality is not normal, it's just common."

Bisexuals are the majority within the LGBTQ+ community, but, in some circles, there is distrust of our sexual fluidity, however broadly or narrowly we embody it. I have noticed that women, straight and lesbian, who are lukewarm in their support of trans rights are often also lukewarm in their belief that bi/pansexuality exists and is not a phase, fetish, symptom of confusion, or punchline.

Have I mentioned how much I hate TERFs? For a while there, it looked like they might successfully co-opt the word "feminism," but in the last few years, I've been heartened to see many younger people of all genders embrace it.

Feminism today considers the cumulative impact of multiple, intersecting factors in a person's systemic oppression, not just gender. It is elastic and expansive, inclusive and never exclusionary. Feminists do not gatekeep womanhood. Feminists do not hurt those more vulnerable; we gather them close, knowing we are stronger together, that "until we are all free, we are none of us free."[1] Feminists do not monitor other people's obedience to society's

[1] attributed to Emma Lazarus

gender roles. We don't believe in that shit! We've always known we were more than society's idea of us.

Identity is self-declared.

It is insulting when, seven years in, someone jokes that I'll eventually admit I'm a lesbian. It is worse when they speculate that maybe I'm not queer at all. I believe others when they tell me who they are. I respect and use their pronouns. I don't consider other people's identities up for debate.

I see gender roles as performance, and by now (age 57) I'm bored. I am attracted to people[2], not genders. You may feel differently! But we have all been growing and expanding our understanding of these issues across our decades of life, right? And especially these last ten years, as homegrown hate threatens to reverse the social progress of our lifetimes and before?

With the privilege I have as a cis white woman, in a country still free enough that she can say she is bi, pan, or queer without fear of imprisonment, I will sizzle

---

[2] honest people; kind people; strong & sexy people; self-aware & healing people; funny people. This list is not comprehensive.

and spit like the red hot fajita dinner special, carried through a country club dining room, past the line of Republican senators at the cold buffet. Watch me make a spectacle of myself, make a mess, whatever it takes, to help others see how complicated this life is, and people are. I want us to stand united against our common enemies.

Until then, watch me sizzle and spit.

EAT ME

I grew like an artichoke, a member of the thistle family, upright and sturdy, with serrated leaves. Each of us grew atop our own stalk. Each was a singular flower with tough, pulpy petals shielding a heart with an earthy flavor, slightly nutty.

Young artichoke-Susan accumulated scars from rough handling but remained mostly intact. Each petal grew from me into a rough, sharp point. By the time I was ripe for harvest, I had layers grown over my heart.

Young artichoke-Susan shifted from purple to green. I became one version of myself and then another, internalizing trauma that was ordinary and everyday.

Mostly, I grew as expected.

Of course I noticed women, over the years, that sizzle of chemistry, but men were always… there. Men were necessary to penetrate these layers, I thought.

The truth is I remain mystified by this life. I bear witness, process slowly. I do not take the reins or the wheel or whatever it is that is taken by the winners who get it – life, that is – unlike young artichoke-Susan.

Or middle-aged artichoke-Susan.

Did you know that an artichoke will sprout a bright purple flower if left too long, unplucked?

When I left my last marriage and its orderly conventions, it was easy bliss with another man that escorted me into the possibility of another life.

I was free to be me, finally.

Then, again, a shift: purple and green to a full spectrum rainbow. Straight to queer and everything beyond; limitless possibility, fluidity; a slur reclaimed, power transferred.

When I first kissed the cheek of the first woman I loved, let's call her the Gardener, I was overwhelmed by the softness of it. She took my face in her hands and kissed me and everything about my life made sense.

Take me apart, I thought. Dismantle me. Peel my tough petals, scrape them with your teeth for whatever I have to offer.

Trust that, deep down, there is a heart worth the trouble.

"I could make us a little veggie garden," said the Gardener. "We could grow artichokes. I noticed you like them. You can compost the petals, you know. They break down slowly," she said, "but I'm patient."

She fixed me with a look and a thrill swooped through me, heart to pussy.

The Gardener knew my layers as her own. She slipped past them with ease. She found my heart and declared it a delicacy, soft and seasoned and, yes, deep down, worth the trouble.

WET DREAM

From my home in the California desert, I feel the watery pull of your lush, green Midwestern valley, as if a river connects us, as if I could ride its current back to you. I remember rain and colorful flowers as I sip coffee and admire my view of dry, rocky formations. I moved to this desert for its open sky, its long, deconstructed views; enough space for me to think and breathe.

But…

On a recent, late spring day, early evening in your city, the humidity built until it burst into a thunderstorm that drove us inside, up to my hotel room on the 10th and top floor. It had tall windows with a river view and a bed with cool, high thread-count sheets.

Multiple rivers drain through this watershed that is your home, coursing through the landscape, as I imagine masculinity travels through you: surging at times, settling into pools, commingling with different tributaries. You are the gentlest radical, shrugging off labels, simply yourself.

We recognize each other.

Back in Joshua Tree, I await the desert spiny lizard who emerges every year around this time; the gopher snakes who slither through the yard; the quail who bustle past with hatchlings in tow. I am at peace, alone in this dry place. It was hard won. But since my visit, since you, my thoughts are damp at the edges, curling with moisture as I remember.

Out of the rain, we peeled off the soaked layers between us and kissed. It felt like an extension of our months-long conversation; easy, intimate, deep. But you were there, in person, and so was I. We touched, after wondering so long. Your energy felt like what I'd imagined.

You knew that I was myself, too.

Outside, the wind picked up. Rain sparkled in the tall windows, reflecting the streetlights below. You saw my queerness, different from yours. But we both understood fluidity. You invited me to dance, or swim, dispensing with expectations and performance. The undeniable passed between us, back and forth, you then me. I tasted your masculine and feminine, both; neither; and something more. Waters ebbed and flowed as, outside, the downpour continued. Lightning lit up the room and then there was a crack and boom of thunder that rolled and echoed.

Tangled up like long lost friends, we watched a rainbow appear and fade away before the light went completely.

That night, beside you, I dreamt of maple trees along a suburban street. I gazed at leaves bright green, swollen and veined, dotted with big, clear drops of rainwater, held by tension, refracting your world.

When I returned to the desert, I brought with me this watery pull, back to you and your green valley, to our fluidity.

I moved to this dry place on purpose, to think and breathe and be alone. But since my visit, since you, my thoughts are damp at the edges, curling with moisture.

&

otherwise

RADICAL

LESS A MAN THAN A GUN

The terrorist wears jeans and a t-shirt, baseball cap: he is twenty-one or -two or -three years old, medium build, straight or curly hair. White skin.

Educated and comfortable and free enough to write promises of hate on the internet, buy a gun or many guns, and stockpile his ammunition.

Born at the turn of the twenty-first century, United States of America. Born lucky. Do not point this out, though, or he will shoot

you

down.

(Really, it is his own death he wants. But he's been thinking a lot, lately, about how good it would feel to kill you.)

He wants you to agree: Men like him should be in charge. He did not get what he was owed. No one listens to him, so now he screams in bullets, fired from an AK-47 style, long-gun rifle, hard as the cock that he – in his defense – was taught to believe meant power.

In the grainy security footage, the terrorist points his gun at strangers and fires with what can only be described as great calm. At last, he is where he belongs.

He has everyone's attention.

When we see him taken alive, we know a black or brown shooter would not survive this. We hope he will explain, make this make sense. (This will never make sense.)

Because by now, he is less a man than a gun.

No, don't dehumanize – listen.

But a gun only says one thing, and that is not a conversation.

As for the lucky white American man? We do not owe him anything. We do not owe him everything, anymore.

I PLEDGE ALLEGIANCE TO NOTHING BUT

that all-seeing, psychic eye, staring from the outskirts of each vulval crevasse, from each puss (see? She understands).

From girlhood to grown, She witnessed our violation, insults heard and felt, not to mention (do not mention) the blood, what it brought and washed away. Of course they do not tell you: a psychic eye watches over every puss (see? Lips parted, She urges speech).

Because She believes you, without question or condition; because She saw everything. The truth is held in our collective, cuntal memory.

I pledge allegiance to the psychic eye, the puss eye.

One day, may we see things Her way.

I DID NOT MEAN TO WRITE THIS
October 2019

I meant to write about young environmental activist Greta Thunberg and her impact, how she was received on her recent visit to the US. I loved how uncomfortable Greta made the "grown-ups," including me. I was dismayed and unsurprised by the sexism chucked at her like crumpled, plastic water bottles: *How dare she not smile?*

But Greta's visit coincided with the final stages of my divorce, and – perhaps you understand? – in that tender time, everything was metaphor.

I read about a funeral held for a seven-hundred-year-old Icelandic glacier that had melted to the point that it could no longer move. It was considered "dead ice."

"I feel ya," I said to a picture of grey rock, all that was left.

Greta got me thinking about damage and denial and when is late too late? "The house is on fire," she said, and it is, but it is also drowning. I watched YouTube videos of glaciers breaking apart, or calving. In one, tourists on the deck of an Alaskan cruise ship startle at the CRACK, then *ooh* and *aah* as one chunk after another of thick blue ice pulls free and collapses into roiling seawater. Some people cheer, others cry out, recognizing the tragedy they are witnessing. I wonder if they feel the spray on their faces, even at their safe distance. I wonder if they know there is nowhere on Earth that is safe. I wonder if they would admit to the thrill of watching the destruction of something beautiful. Or if they'd simply say, "How sad."

If you never join Twitter, does Donald Trump still make a sound? Oh, yes, I'm afraid so. Every day, in that crowded, sweaty, cacophonous room that is Twitter, your President rages and lies and misspells words. He demonstrates that he is neither a great dealmaker nor a good man. We resist and ignore and wish him gone, but we remain frozen in this cruel reality.

But, lately: a promising tremor, as whistle-blows reverberate through ice. Justice moves glacier-slow, but it moves. We are not yet dead ice.

Once the fissure appears, it's just a matter of time before the CRACK.

I did not mean to write about divorce.

Which, in my case, this time, was overdue and bloodless, but still… a casting out, or off; a smack to the bruise of past divisions. The worst: calving from the glacier of my extended family, cousin birthday parties and wedding dances and annual reunions, holiday cards with photos of kids I don't know.

(Sunk deep in that old, familial ice: a Polaroid of me, age fourteen or worse, at one of those family parties, smiling like I wanted to be more like them and less like me.)

When I slipped underwater, the cold was a shock, but I got used to it. I stopped pretending to be frozen.

Who knows, now, in this destabilized climate, what weather will come? Maybe a surprising cold snap, to reshape us, again, hard as ice? On an unseasonably warm day, who knows what seeds might take hold?

Or maybe we will stay fluid forever, curving into experience, slipping through impasse, dancing in eddies that catch, then release us, infused with fresh biology: mineral, animal, botanical.

We must be willing to drown for our transformation, I scribbled one moody night. We must be willing to give ourselves to the cold, dark unknown as we descend and decide: Will I bother to resurface, again?

What has cleaved itself free cannot be reclaimed – thank Nature, if not God. We will grieve for our ruined illusions, of course, even as we wave them goodbye.

I did not mean to write this.

WHAT IS ENDING
December 2021

The month,
the year,
the second year of Covid,
my hope that things will go back to normal. What is ending is my ability to (still) pretend "normal" is not a useless word and concept, that life was not chaotic and hard before, too hard for too many people. Unjust.

I guess what I mean is, I long for a return to the familiar.

I should know better. I wrote it myself, in a novel, six years ago: "No, there is no doubling-back. Life keeps scrolling forward, like a conveyor belt through a factory, but always in one direction, always forward."[1]

Life goes on, so I believed progress

---

[1] *Not On Fire, Only Dying* by Susan Rukeyser (Twisted Road Publications, 2015)

was inevitable. I was sure.

I am no longer sure.

What is ending is a year that began with a violent assault on Congress, the Capitol building, and our Constitutional process. What is ending is democracy, maybe.

And safe, legal abortions.

What is ending is my tolerance for half-assed allyship, polite silence to keep the peace. Spare me that betrayal. Spare me the cowardice of casual bigotry and willful ignorance.

What is ending is my belief that progress will progress as quickly as I wish it would.

My little-girl fantasies of a feminist future… "You and me are free to be"[2] a bit more free, but not equal, not yet. Be patient, little girl, wait your turn, wait for the pendulum to swing back again, again.

Hopefully in my lifetime.

Because I am no longer a little girl but a middle-aged woman who is tired.

What is ending is my will to keep climbing up onto my high horse

---

2 "Free to Be... You and Me" record album and book by Marlo Thomas & Friends, 1972

or even a soapbox
or out of bed, some days.

What is ending is my long-standing habit of pretending I am okay when
I am not okay and
have not been
for a while.

January 6th is what broke me. I wrote about that in order to help purge the trauma – because that is what I do, the only thing that ever helps, I write – and, yes, it was trauma, our collective trauma and grief, shock, and terror, and also we are pissed off, and that takes a toll, too, being pissed off every day for four years and more, and more.

It is terrible, what that man did to us.

What is ending is my patience with anyone who won't admit that much, at least.

Who won't admit that it was trauma when he talked about grabbing pussies and was elected President anyway.

"Indelible in the hippocampus is the laughter," said Christine Blasey Ford, who was disbelieved while Kavanaugh became a Supreme Court Justice.

It takes a toll, it takes a toll. Every woman's pain is mine.

Empathy could save us, save the world, but all the empaths are writhing in lonely agony, holed up and holding themselves in desperate, self-imposed quarantine so that they might survive this; they might survive feeling everything that is ugly, unkind, selfish, and violent. Too many empaths are curled into fetal positions, inside, while outside, their mouths keep smiling through well-meant lies like, "I'm fine, how are you? I'm getting used to this now. It's not so bad now."

What is ending is my ability to smile when I don't mean it. Maybe I am getting used to my mouth settling into a hard, flat line when it is hidden behind an N95 mask. Come, look me in the eyes, if you must know the truth. You will see that what is ending is everything, for all of us, all the time.

ON THE EDGE OF

Lately I'm on edge. You too?

I am preoccupied with sharp things and edges. I'm on the edge of something… not seventeen[1]. I'm closer to seventy (o lord, that is actually true). This meat suit of mine is past its Best By date, but I'm just getting started. Too bad for me that biology beats intention.

I am on the edge of one life and another, another one begun. I live at the middle-aged border of blood, before and after, with all the other, invisible women, liberated women with bills come due. Our aching joints are souvenirs of lives lived, our recklessness survived, if not well. Regret is a badly healed injury that, by end of day, aches and throbs with the old brag of my heart[2].

I live at the edge of poetry and prose,

---

[1] Thank you Stevie Nicks, 1981

[2] Thank you Sylvia Plath, 1963

in a shelter built by dead woman poets, laughed-off lady writers, angry women with broken hearts, women who loved "wrong," and were "wrong," unruly women, braver than me, who wrote the truth and lived the truth, and it cost them.

We all live at the dawn of the world after Trump, after everything we can no longer ignore, after everything we saw and heard and cannot forget.

At the dawn of Don't Say Gay, after Black Lives Matter. After #MeToo.

It was nineteen years ago that Pink sang, "What happened to the dream of a girl president?"[3]

Everything is backwards or the way it has always been.

We are on the edge of blissful ignorance and finally getting it: everything we must question about everything we were taught to believe about race and gender and sexuality and the point of this human life.

We are on the edge of not caring who calls herself a woman, because maybe those of us oppressed one way or the other realize we are fighting over scraps instead of

---

[3] Thank you Pink, 2006

fighting our common enemy. If it's not sisterhood, it is distraction.

We are on the edge of understanding that the enemy is the system we have counted on, all our lives.

There is a thin blue line between
white and Black,
between white and everyone else,
us and them,
(fear)
between good guy and thug,
progress and backlash,
(fear)
between her right to privacy and
his strongly held belief,
between hypocrisy and
the cruelty is the point.

The pendulum swings right and left with so much fucking fear.

Rising among us and into this burning, flooded world is a generation of the future, not our past. Multiracial, exuberantly queer, unencumbered by religion, with a dark sense of humor – because obviously, it's the end of the world! They are radically kind.

All of us clinging by our fingernails to the edge of what used to make sense must agree to let go. Let's go, all at once.

Let's let them drag us to the edge of comfort and over, to whatever awaits us. The freefall through the unknown, the new, may be terrifying, yes. Yes, it will be worth it. I think.

Also, we have no choice.

The opposite of expansion is collapse. Let us survive, if not well.

WITH HER SHARP, HEAVY WORLD

Hampered by mittens, I clutched a tree trunk as the ground shifted. Some animal part of me knew: Earthquake. Like when I felt my first contraction and understood natural obligation.

The red clay hillside, frozen hard as concrete, cracked apart and loosed rocks that bounced across the trail, smashed icy patches from yesterday's snow, and finally tumbled into the ravine's dormant Kudzu. I scrambled towards a shelter further up the trail. Thunder boomed, rain fell in sheets.

If I wasn't on time to pick up my daughter from school, she would panic. Wouldn't she? It was just the two of us. Her father wanted to be free of me more than he wanted her. People offered help, but humiliation drove me South, where I was a stranger.

The shelter was three walls, a roof, and a bench, on which sat an old, heavyset woman. She leaned forward, hands on her knees. Brown skin hung heavy. Silver hair frothed like foam, or clouds.

She muttered.

"Pardon?"

"I said I should've known better. I'm not up for this. Now I'm stuck here, and sick."

"This weather," I said.

The shelter creaked and swayed. It unnerved me, but I didn't want to sit beside her. I left work early, overwhelmed by my cubicle and the people, always around. I checked my cell: no service. I had promised my daughter I was always reachable.

I said, "I need to go."

"Please stay. I'm not well."

"I'm late—"

"It's pouring! We're always late for something, I've learned that much." She regarded me with hazel eyes like tide pools. "I'm a mother too," she said. "I get it. She's fine. They're always fine, until they're not. Then we know how little we control."

Had I mentioned my daughter? I wanted to ask, but my mouth was sealed, as in a dream.

"I'm a storyteller," she said. "I know how to kill time. When the storm is over

we'll walk back, okay?"
She straightened and closed her eyes:

When the last of her children fell to rot, Mother swallowed Earth back down.

The oceans were sour on her tongue. Brown trees scratched the roof of her mouth. The ruined dirt was hot, stinking of plastic. She tasted her rotting children and all the animals. Empty skyscrapers, stadiums and trucks tore at her throat, then fell to her stomach to be dissolved in acid.

Mother had wished her children brave, but always they sought the familiar. At first, she tended them too closely, overcome by love or pity. They all wanted to be boss. Wanted to know who got more. Who didn't pull his weight.

They fought constantly. It wore her down. She spoiled them, but still they would not share. They assumed she would forgive.

Like any mother, she blamed herself.

Now her stomach swelled to bursting with her sharp, heavy world. A storm raged inside, and she knew.

She heaved, brought it all back up.

Earth bobbed into space. Continents shifted into position. The atmosphere glistened with her saliva, pristine again. Roots stirred in clean dirt. Seas teemed with fish already sprouting legs.

Goodbye, she whispered, and a new wind circled the Earth. She left before the hominids appeared.

The strange old woman went quiet, and moments passed in silence. The rain stopped and sun broke through the pines.

Watching a toad leap from a puddle, I unzipped my jacket, suddenly roasting.

I said, "So it's a creation story?"

"Destruction is the important part. When and how to let go, hardest questions for any mother," she said. "It flops on the festival circuit, but I like it. I don't mind ambiguity."

"I have to get my daughter." I tried helping the woman up, but I must've missed her arm. I swiped at air.

"She's fine, I told you. We are in the midst of it, don't you know?"

I walked away. Then ran.

My daughter needed me more than this old woman who maybe was strange? Who maybe didn't move her lips when she spoke?

I wasn't sure, afterward.

I remembered her eyes.

I meant to go back and check on her. Later that day. The next morning. Then too much time passed. She must be okay. Someone helped her.

Of course I was ashamed.

Now I hike this trail every week.

The shelter is empty until I get here. My daughter is grown, gone away from me, toward her own life.

I don't need a lot from people. I need more than nothing, I've learned that much.

"I should have known better," I tell the worried mothers who sometimes pause by me.

WITH HER WITH ME

It settles on me like fog, familiar, turns me
cold, hard, and bloodless, green with
inhaled air pollution.

Envy stabs like hunger
worryworryworry
what if
I can't breathe

Some people can't breathe for real,
Shame on you.

Shame on me, shame in me

It is bitter and sharp, what rises in my throat, then splashes back down where it belongs. Nothing holds me. I am cast out, adrift, forsaken. Of course, because

I am cold, hard, and bloodless, green with
inhaled air pollution.

what if

ALONE, ALONE, ALONE, I grind through gritted teeth. But I can't even have this, not this one little thing, not even despair, because there she is, beside me, like always. Waiting for me to step out from the fog. Patient and kind, she shows our feet at rest on the invisible floor. She trusts it to hold our weight. She paints our nails, *because we deserve beauty,* she speaks without sound.

I do hear.

Her hand on our knee is reassuring. I feel it, but we don't touch. We are the blush of mercy and the loathsome green thing.

Together, the blood rushes back.

With her with me, the fog lifts, as all weather shifts. For some time, we sit only with light.

MY OWN STICKY DUST → BORON → BIG BEAR → SUBTRACTION, RELEASE

MY OWN STICKY DUST

January 2025

Tonight, my dog and I are camped out in my office at the back of the house. Inside, the walls are draped in plastic, and the ceilings are partially scraped clean of their popcorn texture (more accurately: cottage cheese). I wanted to do this when I moved in, eight years ago. There are reasons why it wasn't done before now. But when it's time, you sure know.

This sort of texture was sprayed on to make life easier. It camouflaged imperfections in the drywall: wrinkled tape, lumpy mud. In theory, it absorbed sound. I don't know about that, but my ceilings did absorb light.

I imagined the builders, out here in the Mojave Desert in the late 80s/early 90s, with limited access to supplies.

They probably wanted the house up fast, with minimal fuss. This is a modest, nondescript two bedroom, barely 1,000 square feet. But maybe, when they were freshly sprayed, these ceilings gave the place a funky, contemporary vibe?

(Hmm.)

It occurred to me that the dust collected in this ceiling, near impossible to clean, probably included flakes of skin, shed by anyone (everyone?) who'd spent time here.

"Even a hair could get up there," I said to no one, "if it caught the wind from a door slammed shut."

Dusty DNA clung to my ceiling. I stared at it every day. I called, "How many of you ghosts are up there?"

Earlier today, the man – the angel – doing this work for me said, "They painted it twice."

I knew the texture was harder to remove, once it was painted, and this job was a little worse than he'd anticipated. But then he brightened and said he'd see me tomorrow morning at seven.

This angel-man and apparent early bird does not know how meaningful his efforts are to me, clearing this house of the previous owners' paint, eight years of my own sticky dust, and the ghost DNA of those who stuck around too long because I let them.

Tonight, I said to my dog,

"Sometimes it is necessary to deconstruct your own ceiling, what you stare at every day."

Time for dinner, she said back, with her eyes.

Change is a mess. But when it's time, you sure know.

→ MY OWN STICKY DUST → BORON → BIG BEAR → SUBTRACTION, RELEASE

BORON
July 2021

I drove from Joshua Tree to an old motel in the middle of the Mojave. I was writing my novel, *The Worst Kind of Girl,* which features a woman who owns (and lives in) the fictional Hi-Dez Motel in Yucca Valley. The Boron Motel was the sort of place I had in mind when I imagined the Hi-Dez: mid-century, single story, with a neatly preserved stone veneer exterior. Its neon sign now touts free WiFi. The rooms are clean and functional, updated with a jumble of furniture.

I decided to spend a couple of nights there, alone, to absorb details of desert motel life that would enrich my manuscript. It was the sort of thing I had done before, while writing my first novel, *Not On Fire, Only Dying,* when I revisited New

York's Hudson Valley, where that book is set.

But I forgot that I was no longer that strong woman, bold and independent.

Boron is a small, unincorporated community, rising up out of the desert between Barstow and Bakersfield. It is home to California's largest open pit mine.

"Deposited millions of years ago, borates are crystallized salts that contain boron. Boron is a mineral essential to plant growth, so it is used in fertilizers, but it is also used in high tech applications, such as the heat-resistant glass for smartphones, materials for renewable energy…" and more[1]. Down the road is Edwards Air Force Base.

I was nervous, two hours away from the woman I loved who, I thought, loved me. (She told me she did, all the time.) I did not go out much, alone, anymore. It was easier to let her drive.

I forgot, when I planned this trip. I forgot a lot, when I was writing, lost in words, distanced, detached.

I needed her. Didn't I? She was

---

[1] Rio Tinto website, California operations. www.riotinto.com

patient and kind. Or, she used to be. She was having a hard time. Sometimes I was afraid of her anger, which arrived one day and never left. But I knew it was a lot, dealing with me. I was never satisfied, always wanting to talk. It felt like hatred, what I heard in her voice, but she said that was my anxiety talking, my unhealed childhood trauma.

Everyone said she was patient and kind, so maybe I *was* going crazy?

Lately, my anxiety was worse: Trump, Covid; but I knew it was more than that. My hips ached so badly, sometimes I could not walk. They hurt less when I was curled up like a fetus.

The sun bore down on Boron's sand and asphalt. I went for a drive, a break after writing all morning. In every direction, roads stretched into the distance: wide, flat, no landmarks for a stranger. I tried one that ended at a solitary, partially collapsed Joshua tree. Beyond, there was nothing but desert. I took a picture, already knowing I'd delete it. I got back in my car and drove.

Somehow, I ended up on a four-lane highway with construction barricades, no shoulder. I was trapped before I knew what was happening. I panicked. I desperately wanted out, but the truck behind me followed close, so I stepped on the gas, like I was not driving myself even faster in the wrong direction.

Finally, I saw a turnout and a chance to U-turn. *Thank you thank you thank you,* I whispered, my knuckles white from my grip on the wheel. My heart thumped. I'd been holding my breath. I was finally headed in the right direction, but I thought, *I can't do this. I need help… I need her.* (She told me I did, all the time.)

How the hell did I come to this?

Up ahead was a Burger King. I ate fries in my car: warm ketchup, greasy salt; familiar. I called the woman I loved, embarrassed. I was an adult. I planned this trip. I used to be a strong woman, bold and independent, but now…

She was patient and kind. She stayed on the phone with me until I was back at the motel. I told her I couldn't do it, otherwise.

MY OWN STICKY DUST → BORON → BIG BEAR → SUBTRACTION, RELEASE

BIG BEAR
June 2025

Ascending the Cougar Crest trail, on the north shore of Big Bear Lake, I hiked a path that grew steep and narrow, twisting around tall trunks of cedar; western juniper; and pine: ponderosa, sugar; "gentle" Jeffrey. Lizards darted across the path; a rattlesnake slipped into the shade beneath a canyon live oak. The trail was so rocky, my feet began to ache in their trail runners. I never did anything about that neuroma in my left foot, that tangle of nerves gone numb. Human beings are built to ignore and adapt to pain, I told myself, again.

Today, in Big Bear, my legs felt weak. I was still recovering from allowing myself to wither, physically. Words had broken me as they had saved me, other times. That was how hard I listened to those I loved.

For years, I was frozen, numb as my foot.

This morning, on this hike, my legs reminded me how good strength feels. Hiking was always my meditation, my worship: *Step, step; Step, step*. I was suddenly so grateful for my legs and how they carried me. I started listing other things I was grateful for.

My hips began to ache, a little, reminding me that they usually did not, anymore. I decided to ignore it. Adapt. What was important was that I had my own two legs back under me.

And I had Advil in the car.

I forgot, for a while, that I had always carried myself, at times uphill, navigating rocky terrain, sometimes off-trail and lost for real. I always found my way back. I forgot that a strong woman enacts strength as the wind fills a sail.[1]

Finally, Big Bear Lake came into view, far below. My body was rosy with

---

[1] "Strength is not in her, but she/ enacts it as the wind fills a sail." - Marge Piercy, "For Strong Women"

circulation. My breath swirled through me.

I forgot, for a while, that I was a woman enacting strength and also the wind that moves her.

MY OWN STICKY DUST → BORON → BIG BEAR → SUBTRACTION, RELEASE

SUBTRACTION, RELEASE

July 2025

Six months later, the angel-man returned to paint the walls of my house, all of them. This is a small house, but it was still a big job. After eight years, I wanted my gaze to settle on new, clean walls. No more fingerprint smudges from former friends; no more picture hanger holes, where I took down photographs. No more old, sticky dust.

The previous owners chose to alternate three paint colors throughout the house: gray-green, gray-beige, gray-yellow, creating a dull yet chaotic patch-work.

But also.

These walls held the echo of every conversation since I moved in. When I pressed my ear against their paint, I heard words meant to hurt, meant to embarrass. From someone I loved? Who, I thought, loved me? (Hadn't she told me she did, all the time?)

My dog and I were back in my office, camped out. The angel-man brought two helpers, and they moved quickly through the house, covering the main areas with a bright, creamy ivory that connected and sealed what had been fragmented. The eggshell finish reflected light.

For the kitchen, I chose a bolder hue, the brilliant blue of this desert sky, eye-throb bright, the color that seduced me out here, across country, from the Atlanta area, where I had lived happily, mostly, for eleven years. This desert's blue sky was a high I chased from the moment I first saw it.

To prepare for the angel-man, I cleared away everything: every memento of my life before and since Joshua Tree. I packed up books, took down art. It became editing. I held each item: *How did it feel? Was it worth holding onto? Was it mine, anymore?*

It became a process of subtraction. The less I had, the more I saw.

When the man, (who was not really

an angel, but a kind, hardworking immigrant), flew off to save another, I began the process of putting everything back, but thoughtfully. A curated selection was returned to tabletops and bookshelves. Everything was dusted and wiped clean. Already, the air felt different. I pulled out the brass incense burner I got sometime in the early 90s, somewhere I lived that was not home. I lit a tiny brick of juniper incense and closed the openwork lid. Smoke snaked out through the holes. I walked slowly through the rooms of my house with the burner, the smoke engulfing me, until everything smelled sweet and earthy. Then I opened the windows, and the desert wind gusted in, swirling with the scented air.

I stood in my little living room, before my beloved view of dry mountains, and felt gratitude for new paint and kind people, for wet dreams of possibility. I breathed in deep and exhaled, happier than I had been in a while, maybe years.

The air in here, in me, was clear.

I was home.

ACKNOWLEDGMENTS

"Another Version of Myself" is excerpted from the author's novel, *The Worst Kind of Girl* (Red Light Lit Press, 2025), used with permission.

"You Were the Girl Who" and "With Her Sharp, Heavy World" were previously collected in the author's chapbook, *Whatever Feels Like Home,* (above/ground press, 2021).

"For Sale: Black & Blue Babydoll" and "For Sale: Baby Shoes, Very Worn" first appeared in the author's chapbook, *Swap/Meet* (Space Cowboy Books, 2018).

The following work first appeared as noted: "A Hymn for Us Heretics," (Unleash Lit #1, 2022); "A Story of Blood Through Me," includes an excerpt from "Our Bloody Secrets" (MER Literary Vol. 10, 2012); "Beauty Stuff," produced as part of L Akinyi's short film, "Masks + Mirrors," 2023; "I Didn't Mean to Write This," (XRAY Literary Magazine, 2020); "ID, Please," performed at Out Loud Long Beach, 2019; later adapted for *The Worst Kind of Girl*; "The Proof in Her Gut," (Identity Theory, 2023); "With Her Sharp, Heavy World," (A-Minor Magazine, 2014); "With Her With Me," in response to the painting "Sitting with my Shadow" by Zara Kand (The Green Lady Booklet, 2021)

SUSAN RUKEYSER

writes and lives in Joshua Tree, California. She created the Desert Split Open for literary work that is feminist, queer, and otherwise radical. Her new novel is *The Worst Kind of Girl* (Red Light Lit, 2025). Her debut novel, *Not On Fire, Only Dying,* is from Twisted Road Publications. Susan's short prose appears in many wonderful places, online and in print, most recently, "Writers Resist," and is collected in *Whatever Feels Like Home* (above/ground press, 2021) and *Utility Location* (Bottlecap Press, 2022). As World Split Open Press, Susan publishes select feminist titles, like this one.

www.susanrukeyser.com

www.ingramcontent.com/pod-product-compliance
Lightning Source LLC
Chambersburg PA
CBHW050416110726
47899CB00008B/2744

* 9 7 9 8 9 9 9 3 3 4 3 0 5 *

All I hope for us, as writers and people, is that we stay defiant.

I hope you will not tone it down or watch your language. Promise me you won't self-censor, that you will not obey in advance.

Tell me you won't avoid "bad" words, "sensitive" subjects, or "controversial" takes.

Now, more than ever, you must write into discomfort and say what you mean, what we need to hear.

From the Introduction, ALL I ASK (PROMISE ME)

$14.00
ISBN 979-8-9993343-0-5
51400>
9 798999 334305

A YEAR OF SHORT FICTION

STONE'S THROW

FROM ROCK AND A HARD PLACE

2025

ЯHP